Contest
CRAZY

by Alan MacDonald
illustrated by Judy Brown

PiCTURE WiNDOW BOOKS
Minneapolis, Minnesota

Editor: Jill Kalz
Page Production: Brandie Shoemaker
Art Director: Nathan Gassman
Associate Managing Editor: Christianne Jones

First American edition published in 2007 by
Picture Window Books
5115 Excelsior Boulevard
Suite 232
Minneapolis, MN 55416
877-845-8392
www.picturewindowbooks.com

This Americanization of CONTEST CRAZY was originally published in
English in 2002 under the title YUMMY SCRUMMY by arrangement with
Oxford University Press.

Printed in the United States of America.

Library of Congress Cataloging-in-Publication Data
MacDonald, Alan, 1958–
Contest crazy / by Alan MacDonald ; illustrated by Judy Brown.
p. cm. — (Read-it! chapter books)
Summary: The twins, Ben and Clare, love to enter contests, but when one
of them finally wins, it puts a strain on their relationship.
ISBN-13: 978-1-4048-3134-6 (library binding)
ISBN-10: 1-4048-3134-7 (library binding)
[1. Twins—Fiction. 2. Brothers and sisters—Fiction. 3. Contests—Fiction.
4. Sharing—Fiction.] I. Brown, Judy, 1962– , ill. II. Title.
PZ7.M145 Co 2006
[Fic]—dc22
2006027262

Table of Contents

Chapter One 5

Chapter Two 8

Chapter Three............................ 18

Chapter Four 20

Chapter Five 28

Chapter Six............................... 40

Chapter One

Some twins are hard to tell apart.
Ben and Clare weren't those kind
of twins. For starters, Ben was a
boy, and Clare was a girl. Ben had
freckles; Clare didn't. Ben had fair
hair; Clare had brown hair. Clare
liked to paint her nails pink; Ben
didn't. It was easy to tell them apart.

5

The twins were like most brothers and sisters. Sometimes they played together, and sometimes they argued. But there was one thing they agreed upon—contests. They were both crazy about contests.

It was amazing where you could find contests if you looked. They weren't just in magazines.

They were on cereal boxes, tubes of toothpaste, and bags of chips, too.

Ben and Clare often entered six or seven contests each week.

Ben said that if you entered enough contests, you had to win something eventually. It was only a matter of time.

As it turned out, he was right.

Chapter Two

One Saturday afternoon, the twins were sitting in the kitchen. They had a big pile of contest entry forms in front of them. At that moment, they were considering a contest to win a red sports car. (The twins were too young to drive, but they thought it would be fun when they got older.)

Their mom came over to the table and dropped two Wibble chocolate bars in front of them. "A little treat," she said, "to help you think."

"Thanks, Mom!" cried the twins. Both of them grabbed the chocolate bars at the same time. They started to tear them open.

Luckily, Ben spotted something before it was too late.

"Wait!" he said. "There's some writing on this wrapper. It's some sort of contest!"

Clare looked and saw that he was right. On the wrapper, in big red letters, it said: WIN YOUR OWN WEIGHT IN CHOCOLATE! SEE INSIDE.

The twins stared at each other, speechless with excitement. This was the contest of their dreams.

Both of them were crazy about chocolate. If they had their way, they would have chocolate for breakfast, lunch, and supper. Who needed a sports car? This was a contest they had to enter.

Ben and Clare tried to imagine the size of all that chocolate. One thing was for sure; it would be HUGE!

Carefully, Clare peeled off the wrapper and read the contest rules.

"In no more than 10 words, say why Wibble's chocolate is the best," she read.

"That's easy," said Ben. "'It's yummy.' That's only two words."

Clare wrinkled her nose. "It has to be clever, Ben," she said. "You can't just say, 'It's yummy.' Besides, 'scrummy' sounds much better."

"OK. 'It's yummy and scrummy,'" said Ben.

"That's good. Plus, it rhymes," said Clare. "Wait a minute." She chewed on her pencil, thinking.

"It's yummy and scrummy … and it's going in my tummy," she said with a laugh.

That sounded good. She wrote it down on the entry form.

Wibble's chocolate is the best because:

it's yummy
and scrummy … and
it's going in my tummy

"Ten words exactly," said Clare. "It's perfect."

Next, contestants had to write their name, address, and weight.

Usually, Ben and Clare took turns entering their names for a contest. Ben said it was his turn this time.

"No," argued Clare. "Your name was going on the sports car entry form. So it's my turn."

"I don't want my name on that one. I want my name on this one," said Ben stubbornly.

"All right. I know how to decide," said Clare. She gave a sly smile. "We'll see who is the heaviest."

"What does that have to do with anything?" asked Ben.

"It's obvious, noodle," said Clare. "You win your weight in chocolate. So, the more you weigh, the more chocolate you get!"

"Oh," said Ben. "I never thought of that."

They both raced upstairs to the bathroom. Ben got there first and jumped on the scale. He weighed 48 pounds (22 kilograms). But when Clare stood on the scale, she weighed 55 pounds (25 kg).

"Cheater! You knew that all along," said Ben.

Clare just made a face. In the end, it was her name and weight that went on the entry form.

Chapter Three

They sealed up the envelope and took it to the mailbox.

"I'll mail it," said Ben.

"We'll both mail it," said Clare. "Maybe it will bring us luck."

They both took one corner of the envelope and pushed it into the slot.

"Do you think we'll win, Clare?" Ben asked.

"Well, there's always a chance," said Clare.

Ben and Clare had said that lots of times before. They had entered hundreds of contests. But they had never won anything, except a measly set of felt-tip pens.

"Suppose we did win," said Ben. "We'd share the prize, wouldn't we? I mean, we entered together."

"Of course," said Clare. But as she said it, for some reason, she crossed her fingers behind her back.

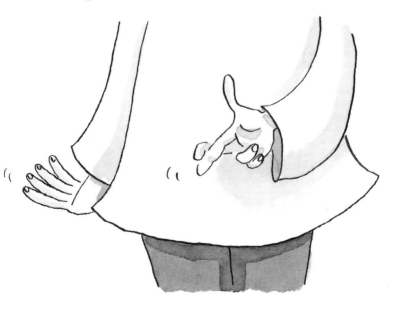

Chapter Four

The weeks went by, and the twins forgot all about Wibble's chocolate bar contest. Then, one Friday evening, the doorbell rang.

Ben opened the door to find a well-dressed woman outside. Behind her stood a man with a camera.

The woman gave Ben a big, friendly smile.

"Hello! Does Clare Mimms live here?" she asked.

"Yes," said Ben. "She's my sister."

"Lucky you," said the smiling woman. "Can you get her for me? She's won a prize."

It took Ben about three seconds to dash upstairs and fetch Clare.

His mind was racing. He tried to remember which contests they had entered recently. What kind of prize had Clare won?

Mom joined them at the door to see what was happening.

"My name is Diane," the lady began. "I'm from Wibble—"

"Wibble?" said Clare. "The chocolate makers?"

"Yes," Diane said, "and I'm delighted to say you've won our contest, Clare. We loved your slogan. It's yummy and scrummy—"

"And it's going in my tummy!"
shouted Ben and Clare.

"That was it," said Diane. "Now,
if you all stand back, we'll bring in
Clare's prize."

A large red van stood outside their
house. Two men were unloading
something from the back.

It was the biggest chocolate bar the twins had ever seen. It was almost as big as the front door. The giant Wibble bar was wrapped in shiny red paper. The delivery men wheeled it into the house on a dolly.

"Oh, my goodness!" said Mom, admiring the huge bar.

"Check it out! It's bigger than me!" shouted Ben.

"I won! I won! I won!" shouted Clare, dancing around the room.

"It weighs exactly as much as you do, Clare," said Diane. "If you'll just stand next to it, we'll take a photo for the newspaper."

Clare stood with one arm around her prize and a huge grin on her face. Ben felt he should have been in the photo, too.

But he wasn't asked.

At last, all of the visitors went away, and Ben, Clare, and their mom were left alone. Clare put the giant Wibble bar on the sofa.

They all looked at it. No one spoke for a while.

"Well! What are you going to do with it?" asked Mom at last.

"That's easy," grinned Ben. "We're going to eat it. Aren't we, Clare?"

Clare said nothing.

Chapter Five

After supper, Clare counted the squares of the chocolate bar. She felt them through the wrapper. There were 72. Clare figured that the bar would last about 10 weeks if she ate one square a day.

Of course, if she shared the bar with Ben, it would last only five weeks. She wasn't sure that she wanted to share her prize.

"Let's dig in," said Ben eagerly.

"No," said Clare. She wasn't ready to tear open the shiny red wrapper. It looked too perfect.

That was the trouble with Ben. He wouldn't save anything. He'd rip off all the paper right away. Then he'd stuff himself with so much chocolate that he'd probably get sick.

"It's not up to you," said Ben.

"Yes, it is," replied Clare. "It's my prize. I won it."

"It's mine, too," said Ben. "It's *our* prize. You promised to share."

"Maybe I changed my mind," said Clare. She hadn't meant to say that. It had just come out. She knew she wasn't being fair, but Ben was starting to annoy her.

This was her prize, the only prize she'd ever won in her life. She wasn't going to let her brother spoil it.

Ben screwed up his face like a baby and started waving his arms.

"That's not fair! You promised, Clare!" he shouted.

"If you must know, I had my fingers crossed. So it doesn't count," replied Clare. "Besides, my name is on the winning entry form."

"It could've been my name on there," argued Ben.

"But it isn't," hissed Clare. "It's my prize, and they gave it to me. I can do what I like with it."

She grabbed the giant bar and dragged it out of the room.

"I'll get you back for this!" Ben yelled after her.

It took a lot of effort to get the bar upstairs and into her bedroom, but in the end, Clare managed it.

Clare didn't come out of her room all evening. She laid the giant Wibble bar on the floor. She was feeling a little guilty about Ben.

She thought maybe she should give in and let him have a piece of her chocolate. But that would mean tearing open the shiny wrapper, and Clare wasn't ready to do that yet.

Later, she told herself, she would let Ben have a piece—later, but not yet. If she ate just one piece a day, she could make it last for a long time.

Her brother, meanwhile, was sulking in his room. He wasn't speaking to her.

When Ben met Clare going into the bathroom, he glared at her.

Clare brushed her teeth and got ready for bed.

She went to sleep with the giant
Wibble chocolate bar on the floor
next to her bed.

In the middle of the night, she
woke up in a panic. She'd been
having a terrible nightmare.

In her dream, Ben sneaked into her
room while she was asleep. Then he
ate all of the chocolate.

"I told you I'd get you back," he said with a smile, chocolate smeared all around his mouth.

Clare switched on her bedside lamp. To her relief, the giant Wibble bar was still on the floor, unopened.

She got out of bed and picked it up. After her nightmare, she wanted to hide her prize in a safe place.

She opened her closet, but it was jammed with clothes and shoes. There wasn't room for a king-size chocolate bar.

Clare sat down on her bed and looked around the room. She saw a narrow gap between her bed and the wall. It looked just wide enough to hide a giant chocolate bar.

When she tried it, the bar slid neatly into the gap between the bed and the radiator. Clare's hiding spot was perfect.

Once Clare adjusted her quilt, no one would know that anything was there.

Back in bed, she smiled to herself. Her treasure was safe. Ben would never think of looking in her secret hiding place.

Chapter Six

In the morning, Clare woke up
and looked on the floor. Then she
remembered where she'd hidden the
giant bar last night. She felt hungry.
Should she have some now, or save it
until after school?

Maybe she'd just steal the tiniest
piece now, to see what it tasted like.

She could hear her mom and her
brother downstairs in the kitchen.

It was safe to get the bar out.
The more she thought about the
chocolate, the more she longed to
taste it.

She imagined peeling back the
red wrapper. She imagined the snap
the chocolate would make when she
broke off the first piece. Would it
taste like ordinary milk chocolate?
Or would it be better? Would it be
sweeter and creamier?

Clare felt down the side of the bed
with her hand.

But instead of feeling the bar, her hand touched the hot radiator. A horrible thought crossed her mind.

She leapt out of bed. Her bare feet felt sticky. Looking down, she saw the carpet was covered in something thick and brown. There was a strong, sweet smell in the room—a smell like melted chocolate!

Clare got down on her hands
and knees and felt under the bed.
Her hand came out coated with
a brown, gooey mess. Under the
bed, she could see the bar's shiny
red wrapper, crumpled and empty.
Chocolate ran down the radiator and
oozed in waves across the floor.

"No!" Clare wailed. "My beautiful
prize! Oh, no, NO!"

Mom and Ben heard her cries and ran upstairs. When they burst into the room, Clare was still on her hands and knees. She was trying to scoop the pounds of melted chocolate back into the wrapper.

"Ugh!" said Ben. "What's all this stuff on the floor?"

"My chocolate bar!" moaned Clare. "It melted on the radiator!"

"What?" said her mom. She looked down in horror at the carpet. "Clare, what made you leave it by a hot radiator?"

"It wasn't hot last night," whined Clare. "I just wanted to hide my prize from Ben."

Ben looked down at his sister. She had chocolate all over her pajamas, chocolate sticking to her fingers, chocolate in her hair, and a big blob on the end of her nose.

He burst out laughing. "I thought you wanted to eat it," he grinned, "not wear it!"

Later that day, Clare knocked on Ben's bedroom door. Ben was on his bed, reading a comic. He didn't look up when Clare walked in.

Clare took something out of her pocket. She dropped it into his lap. It was a chocolate bar—a Wibble's chocolate bar.

"I know it's not the same as the big one," said Clare. "But I just wanted to say I'm sorry."

Ben slowly tore off the wrapper. "I suppose we could share it," he said.

Clare smiled, but Ben wasn't looking. He was staring at the wrapper in his hands.

"Wait a minute," he said. "There's another contest on here!"

Look for More *Read-it!* Chapter Books

The Badcat Gang
Beastly Basil
Cat Baby
Cleaner Genie
Clever Monkeys
Disgusting Denzil
Duperball
Elvis the Squirrel
Eric's Talking Ears
High Five Hank
Hot Dog and the Talent Competition
Nelly the Monstersitter
On the Ghost Trail
Scratch and Sniff
Sid and Bolter
Stan the Dog Becomes Superdog
The Thing in the Basement
Tough Ronald

Looking for a specific title? A complete list
of *Read-it!* Chapter Books is available on our Web site:
www.picturewindowbooks.com